GRIMWOOD

celebrated
WORLD BOOK DAY
2022
with this gift from a
local bookseller and
Simon & Schuster

You're
welcome!

For all the teachers.

First published in Great Britain in 2022
by Simon & Schuster UK Ltd

1 3 5 7 9 10 8 6 4 2

Simon & Schuster UK Ltd
1st Floor, 222 Gray's Inn Road, London
WC1X 8HB

www.simonandschuster.co.uk
www.simonandschuster.com.au
www.simonandschuster.co.in

Simon & Schuster Australia, Sydney
Simon & Schuster India, New Delhi

A CIP catalogue record for this book is available from the British Library.

PB ISBN 978-1-3985-0967-2
eBOOK ISBN 978-1-3985-09665

Printed and bound by CPI Group (UK) Ltd, Croydon, CR0 4YY

WORLD BOOK DAY

World Book Day's mission is to offer every child and young person the opportunity to read and love books by giving you the chance to have a book of your own.

To find out more, and for fun activities including our monthly book club, video stories and book recommendations visit **worldbookday.com**

World Book Day is a charity funded by publishers and booksellers in the UK and Ireland.

World Book Day is also made possible by generous sponsorship from National Book Tokens and support from authors and illustrators.

Greetings!

My name is

ERIC DYNAMITE

and though I may look like a humble woodlouse, I'm also your guide and friend. Welcome! Take off your coat, grab a chair, do a little dance and sit yourself down.

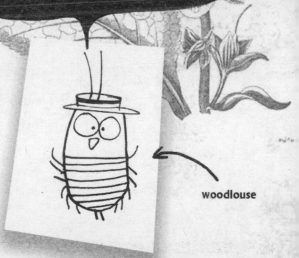

woodlouse

First of all, I'd like to wish you a very happy **WORLD BOOK DAY!** (Unless you are reading this before World Book Day, in which case I'd like to wish you a very happy **DAY BEFORE WORLD BOOK DAY!!!**)

(Or maybe you are reading this after World Book Day, in which case I'd like to wish you a very happy **DAY AFTER WORLD BOOK DAY!!!!**)

Anyway, the main thing I wanted to say is **WELCOME TO GRIMWOOD!** Grimwood sits deep, deep, deeeeep in the countryside. At least I think it does. If I'm honest I've never actually been there. But it is most definitely a **WOOD**, which means it's full of **TREES**. You know, those big things made up of old pencils. There are also, um, leaves. And mud! And stones! And occasionally squashed up fizzy-drink cans. All the wonders of nature are there, oh yes.

I suppose I should introduce you to some of the animals who live in Grimwood, just in case you haven't met them before. Do wash your hands afterwards, though. We don't know where they've been.

STARRING:

A cute little fox from the Big City who thinks everything in Grimwood is amazing. He likes theatre, smelling flowers and everything being great.

Ted's older sister, a streetwise fox who thinks Grimwood is utterly bananas. She likes her mobile phone, growling and looking after Ted.

Bouncy and ferocious, Willow the rabbit has a big heart and endless energy, but she will thwack you in the face if you call her cute, OK?

TITUS!

The mayor of Grimwood. Titus is a kind old stag who is good at baking and cries at soppy films about dolphins. Wants everyone to be lovely to each other.

INGRID!

An extremely glamorous duck who used to be in the movies. Owns a global chain of luxury hotels but currently lives on a pile of old shopping trolleys.

FRANK!

A grumpy owl with massive eyebrows who secretly likes everyone. He spends his evenings reading difficult novels and listening to jazz.

Righty-ho, campers, enough of my witterings. Let's catch up later, yeah? Yeah. Yeah? Yeah? OK then, toodley-pip and goodbyeeeeeeeeeeeee!

PROLOGUE
The Great Capering

It was a warm spring afternoon in Grimwood, and Ted was woken from a deep, delicious sleep by his best friend, Willow the bunny. She was slapping him in the face with a giant kipper.

FLIP FLUP FLOP!

'Ow, ow, ow! Stop!' he cried.

'Wake up, wake up!' hooted Willow, hopping up and down on his chest. 'For 'tis the night of the Great Capering!'

Ted rubbed his paws over his snout.

'The What Whatering?' he said.

'The Great Capering!' repeated Willow, waving her kipper in the air. She grabbed his paws and started to pull him out of his dark and cosy den.

Ted's big sister, Nancy, groaned from her bed and covered her head with a pillow.

'Keep it down, you horrible brats,' she grunted.

'Sorreeeee!' trilled Willow, not sounding sorry in the slightest.

Ted allowed himself to be dragged into the daylight by his hoppity pal. He yawned, stretched his arms and took a deep breath. After growing up in the smog of the Big City, Ted still loved gulping down the fresh air of the countryside.*

YAAAWN

When Ted first arrived in Grimwood, he had imagined that it would be full of kindly bears falling into honeypots and wise old badgers picnicking upon the riverbank. But Grimwood wasn't that kind of place. At first glance, it looked like any old forest. There were trees and earthworms and grassy hills and muddy bits. There were daisies and pine

*You can read ALL ABOUT the WILD adventure of how Ted and Nancy got to Grimwood from the Big City in another book called, er, Grimwood. Available in all good bookshops RIGHT NOW, oh yeah!

cones and massive logs all over the place.

But after a while, he realized that there were also abandoned shopping trolleys, flying squirrels, badgers in Jeeps and a giant electricity pylon called the Magic Tower that buzzed and crackled and filled Grimwood with a most peculiar energy. It wasn't quite what they had been expecting, but Ted and Nancy had grown to love it.

'Here you go!' chirruped Willow, placing a crown of daisies on Ted's head. 'Everyone needs to look their best for the Great Capering.'

'When will you tell me what the Great Capering is, please?' asked Ted.

'It's a festival we hold to celebrate the coming of spring and stuff,' said Willow wrapping a shawl around herself. 'And it's today! We all get dressed up in AMAZINGLY weird clothes and march up to the top of the hill.'

'O-kaaaaaaaay . . .' said Ted.

'And then we set fire to a giant rabbit made out of twigs,' continued Willow.

'WHAT?' Ted gulped.

Suddenly, the friends were interrupted by a very strange noise. Imagine the kind of noise you'd get if an elephant accidentally slammed its trunk in a car door. Yeah, it was that kind of noise.

16

KKBBBRRRRPAAAAAAAAAAAAAAAAARPPP!

Ted screamed. A tall figure wearing a long black cloak staggered towards them.

'Hello, little ones!' bellowed the mysterious creature.

'Hey, Titus,' said Willow casually. 'I see you've dusted down the old bagpipes again.'

'I'm SO excited,' beamed Titus, and he gave the bagpipes another big parp.

'Oh, hello, Ted!' he added. 'Don't be alarmed.

I always get my bagpipes out on the day of the Great Capering. It's the only time I'm allowed to play them in public! After all, I am the mayor.'

Ted took his fingers out of his ears and stared quizzically at the smiling stag. 'What happens after you set fire to the massive wooden rabbit?' he asked.

'Ooh, then it's my favourite bit!' said Titus. 'We all sit around the fire together and tell each other stories.'

'What kind of stories?' said Nancy, who had skulked out of the den.

'Oh, all sorts of things,' said Titus. 'We take turns passing around the Talking Potato.'

'The *what?*' said Ted and Nancy at the same time.

'The Talking Potato!' said Willow, putting her paws on her hips. 'It's a special potato. And whoever is holding the Talking Potato is the only person allowed to speak.'

'Nancy, we need outfits!' squealed Ted. But Nancy was tough and supercool, so she just scowled.

'Hmph,' she muttered. 'You ain't getting me dressing up like some festival weirdo, no way.'

(Half an hour later.)

'You look brilliant, Nance!' said Ted.

Nancy growled.

'Come on, guys!' hissed Willow. 'Let's go.'

There was a buzz of excitement as all the animals of Grimwood gathered at the base of the hill.

'Look, it's Frank!' said Willow, nudging Nancy and pointing to a large beech tree. Frank was perched at the very top, with what looked like several long, colourful ribbons gripped in his talons. Normally, he would have swooped over for a chat, but today he had a very important job to do.

When Titus gave him a nod, Frank took to the air. As he soared and swooped, the fluttering ribbons made it look like he was painting rainbows in the sky. At the same time, a band of squirrels dressed in sparkly leotards began to gently blow on some pan pipes. They played a single eerie, low note, which gradually grew louder and louder.

Titus was standing on a fallen tree trunk.
He stretched his arms up high, which made
his cape billow dramatically in the wind.

'Grimwood!' he bellowed. 'Salute to the sun!'

Hundreds of paws were raised in the air.

'Cool!' gasped Ted.

Titus closed his eyes.

'We give thanks to the cosmic energy of the Earth!' he cried.

'Thank you, cosmic energy of the Earth!' shouted everyone else.

Then they all held paws and chanted together:

Thank you for the trees!
Thank you for the bees!
Thank you for the fleas
That live upon my knees!
Thank you for the cheese!
Have you seen my keys?
Thank you for the breeze!
And the whys and the zees!

'Um, this is weird,' murmured Nancy.

'Yes, I know! Isn't it BRILLIANT?' said Ted, his eyes wide in wonder.

'Let the Great Capering . . . COMMENCE!' shouted Titus.

There was much clapping and cheering, and the animals trudged up the hill.

Several beavers were already at the top. They were operating ropes and levers and

lowering what looked like a giant wooden rabbit onto a big pile of logs.

Nancy gave a whistle. 'Woah. That is going to make a VERY big fire,' she said.

'How do they light it?' she asked Willow.

'Pamela,' said Willow, nodding at the eagle perched high above their heads.

Pamela lived at the very top of the Magic Tower. Her nest was made from bits of old mobile phones, computers, TVs, satellite dishes and dangerous-looking wires she had collected from goodness knows where.

'PCKAAAAAAW!'

screeched Pamela. She was holding a large burning torch in her beak.

Ted covered his eyes.

There were cheers and gasps as Pamela swooped down and dropped the flaming torch inside the belly of the giant wicker rabbit. Then she swooped back again and flung in what looked like a large barrel of gunpowder. The crowd fell silent. Ted peeked through his paws.

'Has it worked?' whispered Nancy.

KA-
BOOOM!

'You lot love a bit of drama, don't you?' laughed Nancy. 'Why couldn't you just build a nice little bonfire like everyone else?'

'It's tradition!' said Frank, pecking the ribbons from his claws.

'Frank! I didn't know you could do all that dancing and swooping and stuff,' said Ted.

Frank gave a shy grin and then bobbed his head around from front to back in that weird way that owls do.

The music had started up again, and the animals of Grimwood began a long night of feasting and dancing in the flickering firelight. Next to the fire was a circle of logs and tree stumps, and a mushroom called Sally. It was here that Titus sat down.

'Ow!' said Sally, who then died.

'Nothing like resting one's hooves after a long day being mayor,' Titus said to nobody in particular. 'Right! Who's for storytime?'

'We are, we are!' chorused Ted and Willow, jumping up and down.

'Bring it,' shrugged Nancy, settling down with a cup of coffee.

Everyone gathered blankets and cushions and sat in a cosy circle around the flickering flames.

'I'll start,' said Titus. 'What with me being mayor and everything.'

'Aye, that'll be the tenth time you've mentioned it today,' said Frank.

'Get on with it!' quacked Ingrid, as she gingerly placed some cucumber slices on her eyes. 'I have ten minutes until I need to wash this face mask off.'

'Righty-ho!' said Titus.

Hello, everyone! Gather round. That's right, bottoms on logs, fangs in mouths, tails tucked away. Squirrels, no fighting please. Right, where were we? Oh yes, my story. HURRAH!

This is a story about a *very* odd thing that happened to me one day a long, long time ago, before I was mayor. I think. Is it true? Yes. But also no. Yet also . . . yes. Because what is 'the truth' anyway, hmm?

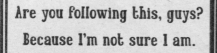

Are you following this, guys? Because I'm not sure I am.

Some of you know that I like to trot through the woods of a morning, collecting berries for my Crazyhorns Power Juice smoothie. And do you know what makes my smoothies taste so extra delicious? That's right – gumberries. Big, juicy, purple gumberries, which grow in clusters on the banks of the Small Pond.

So there I was, happily gumberry-picking, when my hooves got in a tangle and I slipped. My basket of gumberries flew into the air and I fell head first into the Small Pond which, as you know, is not the cleanest sploosh in the world. Plastic bags and tiny dirty fish swam around my head. I gasped for air, waving my hooves around in a panic. I'm a terrible swimmer, and truly, it felt as if I was going to drown.

'Nooooooo!' I cried. 'I'm too beautiful to die!'

Suddenly, I felt two strong arms wrap themselves around me. I was dragged to the banks of the pond and slowly, after much spluttering and coughing, I opened my eyes to see who had saved me.

Imagine my surprise as I came face to face with a deer! A very pretty deer, actually, with long eyelashes and the most delicate snout.

'Thank you so much for saving me!' I gasped.

The deer bowed shyly, and it was then that I noticed the most peculiar thing of all.

From the waist down, the deer was a FISH.

'Good gracious!' I gasped again. 'You're . . .
you're . . . what are you?!'

'I am a merdeer,' it said. 'Half deer, half
mermaid.'

'Holy mackerel!' I said. 'I've never seen
anything like you in my life!'

'I know, I'm pretty special,' said the merdeer,
fluttering its gigantic eyelashes.

'How can I thank you, O mysterious
merdeer?' I asked.

'Ooh!' said the merdeer. 'Will you grant me
three wishes?'

'That seems fair enough,' I shrugged.

'Wonderful,' said the merdeer. 'Oh, and you
can just call me Sandra.'

With that, Sandra dived back underwater.

I'm not sure if it was the bump on the head,
but I still felt dizzy. A merdeer! I hadn't even
known they existed.

Then Sandra popped back up again. She

was holding a toaster.

'My first wish is for you to fix this toaster. Whenever I use it the toast either comes out too floppy, or completely burns and goes black and smelly. It's doing my head in!'

She passed me the toaster. There was a small black dial on the side of it. I carefully turned the dial a little way.

'That should do it,' I said, passing it back.

Sandra looked at me with her beautiful big eyes.

'Thank you! And what is YOUR name, O handsome one?' she asked.

I giggled shyly and snorted, and for one terrible moment a bubble of snot blew out of my left nostril.

'I'm Titus,' I gabbled. 'Titus Crazyhorns. How long have you lived here?'

'It feels like forever,' she said quietly.

'But I'm always foraging for gumberries

33

around here. How have we never met before?'
I asked.

'Well,' said Sandra. 'Actually, we have. Remember the little deer who would flick paint at your antlers in playgroup?'

I gasped, for about the millionth time.

'Silly Sandra the pesky paint-flicker? Is it really YOU?'

Sandra giggled.

'That's me, all right! You see, one day I found this necklace lying in the bull rushes. I put it on and – kablammo! I was instantly turned into a merdeer.'

She pointed to a silvery necklace that was looped around her neck. The pendant looked like a tiny conch shell.

'The necklace did this to you?' I asked.

'Yes!' said Sandra cheerfully. 'Just my luck to pick up a cursed necklace, eh?'

I thought back to when me and Sandra were at playgroup together. She was always getting her hooves stuck in playdough and eating all the red crayons. I suppose if anyone was going to find a cursed necklace and get turned into a sea creature, it was going to be her.

'Now, my second wish,' said Sandra, 'is that you grant me . . . A MILLION MORE WISHES!'

I shook my head sadly.

'My dear Sandra, you seem to be confusing me with a genie, when all I am is a sensitive, hard-working stag who is very good at baking. I'm afraid I can't grant you that wish.'

Sandra seemed disappointed.

'I could, however, make you a delicious Victoria sponge cake?' I suggested hopefully.

'Oh yes, that'll do,' said Sandra.

So I went to the shops to get some flour and eggs, while Sandra did some thinking about her third wish.

When I returned, she reached out her hooves towards me.

'Titus, I wish for you to join me here in the Small Pond,' she said.

'Um, what?' I said.

'Become a merdeer like me! We could laugh and talk and eat dirty little fish together.'

Now, obviously I thought Sandra seemed v nice and everything. But I wasn't sure I wanted to become a merdeer. And I was awfully fond of my legs.

'Hmm,' I said.

'But you promised to grant my wishes!' wailed Sandra.

I had an idea.

'I know, why don't I make your Victoria

sponge cake first. Because once I'm a merdeer,
I won't be able to do earthbound things like
baking any more.'

Sandra thought for a moment.

'Fine. I'll wait.'

I trotted back home as fast as
I could. I needed to bake
the finest cake of my
life. My future
depended on it.

It was dusk
by the time
I wobbled back
to the Small
Pond on my
bike, balancing
the cake in my
basket along
with a pot of tea
and two china cups.

This is
meant to
be a
bike

'Oh, Saaaandra!' I trilled.

Sandra plopped up from the depths of the Small Pond.

I laid a picnic blanket down by the water, so that I could sit next to her, and presented her with the cake.

She clapped her hooves together with delight.

'I'm so sick of eating tiny dirty fish!' she squealed, as I passed her a large wedge of perfectly moist – yet airy – vanilla sponge.

She snaffled it up in one go, so I cut her another slice, and another.

'Oh, Titus! This is the most delicious thing I've ever eaten!' cooed Sandra.

I must admit, friends, it gave me great joy to see her so happy. Soon her snout was covered in cream and jam, and she told me tales of her life in the murky pond.

Eventually, Sandra licked the plate clean of crumbs.

'Well,' I said with a sigh. 'I suppose that's the last time we'll ever get to enjoy tea and cake.'

Sandra looked stricken.

'That's the last time I'll get to eat your cake, *ever*?' she said.

I nodded sadly.

'Are you *sure* there's no way you'd be able to bake underwater?' she sighed.

I shook my head.

Sandra looked even sadder.

'But there is another way,' I said.

'What?' asked Sandra. 'Tell me! I'll do anything to taste more of your delectable baked goods!'

'What if, instead of wishing for me to live out my days with you as a weird sea creature, you wished for me to bring you a cake every week?' I ventured.

'Ooh, it's an idea, isn't it?' said Sandra.

'Yes,' I said. 'Yes, it is.'

And that, my friends, is why for the next twenty years I delivered a wonderful sponge cake to the banks of the Small Pond every week. Until one week . . . Sandra just didn't turn up. Maybe she died. Or maybe she realized if she just took the cursed necklace off, she wouldn't be a merdeer any more. Who knows. But it was one of the most mysterious and romantic times of my life . . . **99**

The End

Titus sniffed and dabbed at his eyes with a handkerchief.

'She died, I reckon,' said Nancy.

'Agreed,' said Willow. 'No other explanation.'

'Unless it was all a load of nonsense,' quacked

Ingrid. 'You lot are all the time coming to my pond and hitting your heads and falling over and being idiots. You think a cake would last five seconds with a load of ducks around? Titus, this was just you being silly from bonking your head in the water.'

'Would make sense,' nodded Frank.

'Oh, you are all BEASTLY,' shrieked Titus. 'Someone else take this ghastly potato then!'

'Me, me, meeeeeee!' yelled Willow, bouncing up and down.

'Anyone?' said Titus.

'MEEEEEEEE!!!!' screamed Willow, pulling at her ears.

'Oh! Willow, I didn't see you there,' said Titus. 'Here you go.'

Ok, guys, I'm going to tell you a story about a thing that happened to me when I was just a baby bunny. Whenever I tell people this story they go, 'no way, that can't be true!' Or, 'go away, Willow, you're being annoying' or, 'get your own biscuits'. But I'm telling you that it IS true.

I was hopping through the forest one evening, digging up radishes. You know those weird, bright pink lumpy ones? Cosmic Knobblers, we call 'em. They are deeeeelicious. Anyway, I was happily bouncing along;

scoffing Cosmic Knobblers, when I saw a weird footprint in a nettle patch. It didn't look like any animal I recognized and it didn't belong to a hoomin.

Willow calls humans 'hoomins', I really don't know why.

I followed the footprints through the nettles, then onto that stony bit past the Small Pond. I was getting further and further away from my home in Bunnyville. Suddenly, I saw something glowing behind a bush.

'Hello?' I said to the glowing bush.

'PWEEEEEEEEE!' it said, which was weird.

I hopped towards it a bit more, and that's when I saw ... AN ALIEN.

It was purple and had massive eyes and really weird feet. When it saw me it made all sorts of excited noises and a green light shone out of its tummy.

I was a little freaked out. But then the alien handed me a card.

> GREETINGS EARTH CREATURE. MY NAME IS CHONKY AND I AM FROM A FARAWAY PLANET. I WILL NOT HARM YOU.

'Oh, cool!' I said. 'Nice to meet you, I'm Willow!'

I held out my paw to shake the alien's hand, and it wrapped a slimy purple tentacle around me.

'Hey!' I said, and tried to pull my paw back, but then all of a sudden I was grabbed by loads of slimy purple tentacles and the alien started to drag me away. Then everything went dark.

The next thing I remember is opening my eyes and finding myself in a room full of strange noises. I realized I was lying down. But when I tried to get up, I couldn't! My paws had been strapped down by some fizzy strawberry laces.

'AAARRRRGH!' I yelled.

The alien scooted over and made more excited *beeping* and *booping* noises. Its tentacles waggled about all over the place.

Then ANOTHER alien popped up next to it.

'AAAAAARGH!' I yelled again.

The second alien held up a machine and pointed it at me. A bar of light passed over my body. Then I noticed a big computer screen next to me. It beeped and said,

'SPECIES SCANNED AND IDENTIFIED: CUTE LITTLE BUNNY-WUNNY'.

'OOOH!' said the aliens.

'Let me go, you horrible nasty cosmic beings!' I yelled.

'There's no need to be rude,' said one of the aliens.

'Oh!' I said, because I was quite surprised that they could talk.

'Do not be afraid, small creature,' said the other alien. 'We will not harm you. We have come from a planet far, far away, which is much more intelligent and fun and brilliant than this smelly old place.'

'Hey!' I said. 'Don't talk about Grimwood like that.'

The alien sighed.

'We are talking about all of Planet Earth,' it said. 'We have come here to collect specimens to take back to our home planet. We have been looking for a cute little bunny-wunny for some time, and we are so excited to have found you!'

The aliens did a brief happy dance and then high-fived each other, which was tricky because they had tentacles instead of hands. So it was more of a high sixteen.

WAHOO!

'Which one of you is Chonky?' I asked.

'Me!' said one of the aliens.

'You tricked me!' I yelled. Freeing a leg, I kicked the alien quite hard in a squidgy bit.

'OW!' said Chonky. 'That wasn't very nice!'

'Well sometimes I am NOT NICE,' I said. 'And I am NOT a cute little bunny-wunny, that's an absolute lie. I am actually quite tough and scary.'

The aliens looked at me and both went 'awwwwww'.

Chonky slithered over carrying a massive jar. He wrote something on a label and stuck it to the glass. It read:

SPECIMEN #1:
CUTE LITTLE BUNNY-WUNNY

The other alien – I never found out its name, so let's just call it Bonky – grabbed my paw.

'Stay still, cute little bunny-wunny,' it said. 'You won't feel a thing.'

I thought it was going to inject me with something weird, but instead it just pressed my paw into some ink and splodged it on a bit of paper. Then it glued my pawprint onto the side of the jar.

'W-what will you do with me?' I stammered.

The aliens looked at each other.

'Honestly?'

I nodded.

'Honestly, we'll probably put you in this jar and then fly back to our planet billions of light years away. And then we'll have a cup of tea.'

My nose twitched.

'That doesn't sound so bad,' I sighed.

'And after the cup of tea, we'll probably eat you,' whispered Chonky.

'WHAT DID YOU SAY?' I shouted.

'Nothing!' said Bonky, kicking Chonky in the tentacles.

I had to think quickly. Suddenly, I remembered I had spent the day eating Cosmic Knobblers. Now, as I'm sure you all know, Cosmic Knobblers have quite a dramatic side effect. They really make you ... well ... they really make you parp. Especially if you eat a lot of them, like I had.

I squeezed my eyes shut, clenched my tail and let out an enormous guff.

The smell made Chonky and Bonky stagger backwards. They put their tentacles over their faces. Chonky started to cry.

'POISON GAS, POISON GAS!' they howled. With one tentacle, Bonky untied me from the table. I hopped down, grabbed the fizzy strawberry laces (because waste not want not) and tried to find an exit from the weird room. But I couldn't see a door. There were just loads of screens and buttons and rows and rows of glass jars.

'Get it off the ship!' yelled Chonky. 'The smell! The smell is melting our braaaaaaains!'

I let out another deadly parp.

'Open the door!' I shouted. 'Or else!'

I menacingly waggled my bottom at them.

Bonky pulled a lever and a hatch in the floor slid open. I hopped towards it, but just before I left I turned around to face the aliens.

'And don't you EVER think about doing that ever again!' I growled.

'You,' said the aliens, between sobs, 'are definitely NOT a cute little bunny-wunny.'

'That's right,' I nodded.

I leapt through the hatch and hopped all the way home. When I told everyone about what had happened, nobody believed me. In fact they said, 'Stop fibbing, Willow. We can smell your parps so we know you've been out secretly eating Cosmic Knobblers. They always make you over-excited. Now go to bed at once, you naughty little rabbit.'

So I did, boo hoo hoo. But not without peeking outside my window first. The forest was glowing and tree branches waved around in the wind. Slowly . . . the alien spaceship rose into the sky and then ZOOOOOOMED off into space. "

The End

Willow took a deep bow.

'Woah!' said Ted. 'What an amazing story!'

'Where can I get some of these Cosmic Knobblers then?' asked Nancy, examining her paws.

'Uncouth and inelegant,' huffed Ingrid the duck, adjusting her silk turban. 'There was simply no need for all that . . . all that . . .'

'Parping?' offered Willow.

'Yes!' shrieked Ingrid, flapping her wings.

'Oh come now, Ingrid, we all release little smelly clouds from time to time,' said Titus gently.

'How DARE you!' cried Ingrid, thwacking him with her vintage handbag. 'I am a lady.'

'You're a duck,' said Nancy flatly.

'I am a lady duck,' scowled Ingrid. 'Roll the vegetable of power towards me, please.'

Ingrid waddled over to the potato, sat on it, and began to tell her story.

'My darlinks, I have lived an amazing life. You don't even know the half of it. I used to live far, far away from these stinky old woods. You know that after my years in theatre, I lived the glamorous life of a Hollywood duck. Fast cars, wild parties, as many brown paper bags of seeds as I wanted.

Was I happy? Yes. I had everything a duck could ask for. But sometimes the strangest adventures find you, even when you are not looking for them.

I lived in a pond that belonged to one of

the most powerful movie stars in Hollywood. One day I was bobbing amongst the reeds, reading the newspaper, when I heard a low *quaaaaaaack*.

I looked up and next to me was a duck in a tie and dark glasses.

'Don't look at me,' she hissed.

I quickly looked back down at my paper.

'You never know when you're being watched,' said the duck. 'Now, Ingrid. Have you ever thought about becoming a spy?'

I tried not to gasp.

'How do you know my name?' I whispered.

The mysterious duck laughed quietly.

'I know everything. I know you read the papers here every morning. I know you had toast and honey for your breakfast. I know your shoe size.'

'But I don't wear shoes,' I whispered.

'I know that too,' she said.

This duck was cool.

'Who are you? Who do you work for?' I whispered.

'You can call me Agent Onions. And I work for important people,' she quacked softly. 'Powerful people. If you join the organization, I can tell you more. But you need to be ready.'

'Ready for what?' I said.

'Ready for action. Ready for secret missions, danger, travel.'

I looked at Agent Onions.

'Do I get a fancy car?'

'Yes, you will get a fancy car,' she said.

'And loads of weapons and gadgets?'

She nodded.

'What about the sunglasses?'

'We will sort you out with some sunglasses.'

She handed me a briefcase.

'Your first mission is inside,' she said. 'Read it, then put it back in the briefcase.'

'This sounds reasonable,' I said.

'The briefcase will explode in sixty seconds,' said Agent Onions.

'ARGH!' I yelled.

But Agent Onions was already gone.

I quickly opened the case and read my mission. It seemed simple enough. I had to find an enemy submarine in the middle of the ocean, steal some important codes and take them directly to the Queen of England.

'Easy!' I quacked. But what was I to do with the briefcase? It was going to explode any second.

Luckily, just at that moment my old friend Herman flew by. Herman was a pelican.

'Here you go, Herman!' I said, and I flung the briefcase into his ridiculously large mouth.

'Yum! Thanks, Ingrid,' said Herman, swallowing it down.

I put my wings over my ears and waited ... and waited ...

Herman gave a little burp.

'Delicious! Got any more?' he asked.

Well, I was very relieved it hadn't exploded

inside Herman's stomach. That would have been terrible.

The next day I found the submarine – it really didn't take long – and the day after that I flew all the way over to England to deliver the top-secret codes to the Queen.

'You are a brave duck indeed!' said the Queen. Then one of her corgis tried to eat me so I had to leave immediately. Still, it had been an honour to serve.

Unfortunately, my time as a spy did not last long. Back in Hollywood, Herman had eaten a large pickled egg and it had somehow triggered the exploding briefcase. It made a terrible mess. There were bits of egg and briefcase and Herman all over the place.

'Sorry about that,' I said to Agent Onions, who seemed quite peeved about the whole thing. Apparently an enemy duck had found some important documents in the exploded briefcase.

'You must leave the country at once,' she said. 'And start a new life.'

A single tear rolled down my beak.

'But I want to be a secret agent for ever,' I sniffed.

Agent Onions patted me on the shoulder.

'Don't worry, Ingrid,' she said. 'As long as you *never* tell anyone about what has happened here, you will still be one of us. As long as, even years from now, you *never* sit around a fire and tell people that you used to be a top-secret spy . . . as long as you NEVER do that . . . then you, and indeed the world, will be safe. **99**

The End

'Oh dear,' said Frank.

'OH NO,' said Ingrid, covering her beak with her wings. 'What have I done?'

'Um . . . I really think we'd best move on,' said Titus, hurriedly. 'Before, um . . . before anyone hears us. OK, so who wants the Talking Potato?'

'Frank, you do one!' said Ted.

'Naw,' said Frank shyly. 'I'm not great at telling stories.'

'Oh PLEEEEEEEASE!' said Willow. 'PLEASEPLEASEPLEASEPLEASE PLEASEPLEASEPLEASEPLEASE PLEASEPLEASEPLEASEPLEASE PLEASEPLEASEPLEASEPLEASE PLEASEPLEASEPLEASEPLEASE PLEASEPLEASEPLEASEPLEASE PLEASEPLEASEPLEASEPLEASE PLEEEEEEEEEEEEEEEASE!'

And, if only to make Willow's screaming stop, Frank perched gingerly upon the potato.

'THE GREATEST
STORY EVER TOLD'
★★★★★

'So, er. Right. An interesting story ... OK. Well, one day when I was a wee owl in the mountains of Scotland, I was flying about and I thought I saw a gold coin poking out from some rocks. So, um, I flew down to take a look. But it turned out just to be a scrunched-up biscuit wrapper.'

The End

Everyone was quiet for a moment.

'Is . . . is that it?' said Nancy eventually.

'I told you, I'm not one for telling stories!' huffed Frank, ruffling his feathers.

'It was great, Frank!' said Ted kindly (and also sweating a lot because he was lying).

'Frank, that was a major fail,' said Willow. 'NEXT!'

Nancy bent down and grabbed the Talking Potato.

'Now this,' she said with a smirk. 'This is a story.'

So I may as well tell you about this thing that happened to me way back in the Big City. Sometimes that place can be dangerous and scary, you know? When I was out and about with my crew on those streets I saw some wild stuff.

My best mates were Bin and Hedge. I found Bin in a bin and I found Hedge in a hedge. We'd roam the streets as a gang cos it was a bit safer and we got more food that way. Obviously we hung out at the back of Speedy Chicken for the good stuff, but there was also

71

GoGo Pizza and Filthy Burgers, and Hedge went mad for the kale smoothies at Green & Lovely. And if we were really smart, we could eat at some of the finest restaurants the Big City had to offer. You just had to know where to look.

The swankiest place in town was called The Golden Moose, where you'd find the best steak and chips you've ever eaten. They'd do little bread rolls filled with salty butter . . . oh man, I am dribblin' just thinking about them. Anyway, the only way to get to the back of The Golden Moose was to climb up this rickety metal fire escape. You had to go right up, and if you didn't like heights you were in trouble cos the restaurant was right at the top of a massive skyscraper.

One night after a long climb, me and the gang clambered over the wall onto the rooftop and sat in the dark for a while, panting. Then we froze. Someone else was up on the roof.

'Groaaaaaaan...'

The noise was coming from a lump in the corner. I went to investigate, snarling a little just in case it was a wrong'un. As I got closer to the figure I couldn't believe my eyes. Slumped there clutching his belly and looking very sad, was . . .

BATFOX.

What do you mean, *who's Batfox?* Everyone knows Batfox! He's a mysterious superhero who fights crime and drives a wicked cool car and wears a mask! And he usually speaks in this really low gravelly voice, but on this particular evening he sounded kinda squeaky.

'My tummy!' cried Batfox. 'Oh, it hurts!'

I frowned. This wasn't standard superhero behaviour.

'Was it something you ate?' asked Hedge.

Batfox nodded weakly.

'A massive load of garlic snails,' he said sadly. 'And then a massive chocolate cake. My absolute faves,

but now I need the toilet really badly.'

He moaned and clutched at his stomach again.

'There, there, Batfox,' said Bin, patting his head. 'I'm sure you'll be all right by tomorrow.'

Batfox sniffled.

'But I'm the hero of the night!' he wailed.

'Baddies will take over the Big City if I'm not around to foil their evil plans!'

Then he covered his face with his paws and started blubbing.

'Chill out, Batfox,' I said. 'We can help you out if you like.'

'Really?' said Batfox, perking up. 'Oh thank you, thank you so much, brave foxes!'

Bin and Hedge shifted about a bit, because to be fair they hadn't said anything about helping, I'd just gone for it.

Batfox started to take off his superhero costume.

'No!' cried Hedge. 'Don't ruin the mystery! Haven't you got a spare?'

'Ooh, I have as it goes,' said Batfox, and he dug around in a rucksack. He nodded at me, handing over a cape and a rubber mask. 'Here you go.'

Well, there's no point lying about it. I put on the gear and I looked very cool indeed.

'They call me . . . THE HOODED PAW!' I boomed.

'Who does?' said Bin.

'Well, nobody yet,' I said. 'But they will do.'

Suddenly, there was a massive light in the sky.

'It's the Batfox signal!' squealed Batfox. 'You must go at once! Someone's in trouble!'

'Er ... OK,' I said. 'Haven't you got any gadgets and gizmos and stuff?'

Batfox threw a belt at me that had loads of things strapped to it. 'That belt has everything you need.'

I scampered over the rooftops as fast as I could, blending into the dark shadows.

I could hear a loud 'duh DUH duh DUH duh DUH' noise, and turned around to see Bin and Hedge running after me, playing dramatic music out of their phones.

'Guys, please,' I said.

Then we saw them. A family of little chihuahuas were trapped on top of a bus shelter, yelping for help.  Beneath them was a pair of huge, nasty-looking dogs, growling and slobbering. I leapt through the air, cape billowing behind me. Everyone gasped as I landed face to face with the horrible hounds.

'Batfox! You came!' squealed the tiniest chihuahua, clapping her paws together.

The dribbling dogs looked me up and down.

They started to laugh.

'You ain't Batfox!' said one of them. 'You're half his size!'

This was true. I made my voice as deep and growly as I could.

'I am The Hooded Paw. Leave the little guys alone, OK?' I said.

The dogs laughed.

'Your voice is RIDICULOUS,' said one of them. 'Say something else, go on!'

'You'd better watch it, or else,' I said.

The dogs were now rolling around on the ground laughing. I got the feeling the chihuahuas were a bit disappointed, too.

'The belt,' hissed Hedge, 'use the belt!'

I fiddled about with the Batfox utility belt, not really knowing how any of the gadgets worked. I picked the biggest button and pressed it, hoping a laser beam would zap the dogs in the face.

But instead, a tiny mirrorball came out and started spinning around. Then out popped a little mouse in sunglasses, who started disco dancing.

'Aaaah!' said everyone.

'How is this meant to fight crime?' I spluttered. I ripped off the rubber Batfox mask and took off my cape.

'You're right,' I said to the dogs. 'I'm not Batfox. He ate too much and is a bit poorly. So I stepped in.'

'I want my money back!' yelped a chihuahua, waving its phone about. 'I sent out a Batfox signal, not a Normal Fox signal!'

'Well I ain't no normal fox,' I snarled. 'I'm Nancy.'

And then –

BIFF! BANG!!

KAPOW!!! SHAZZAM!!!!

I karate-chopped the big dogs' faces clean off! Or at least gave them a bit of a fright. They ran off whimpering, tails between their legs.

'Wow,' said Bin and Hedge. 'They were some cool moves, Nance!'

I helped the terrified chihuahuas get down from the bus shelter.

'You're my hero!' said the smallest one.

'Yeah, Batfox is rubbish. Go, Nancy!' said the second-from-smallest one.

I felt quite chuffed to be honest.

Anyway, there I was soaking up the adoration, when who should roll up? That's right. Batfox.

'Don't panic, everyone! Batfox is in the house!' he announced.

We all stared at him.

I chucked his utility belt on the floor.

'This wasn't much help,' I said.

'Ah, I see you activated the Mouse Disco button,' he said. 'Yes, that would have been useless. What seems to be the problem, fans?'

'Nancy's sorted it,' said Bin.

I buffed my claws and grinned.

'Yes, we're fine now,' said a chihuahua. 'Nancy got rid of the baddies and she didn't need a cape or nuffink.'

Batfox looked a bit miffed.

'Well I've had a peppermint tea and I feel TOTALLY FINE now,' he huffed. 'So, thanks and everything, but I've got it from here.'

I shrugged.

'No sweat, Batfox,' I said. 'You do you. I do me.'

And I gave him a high five.

Then me and Bin and Hedge strutted down

the street, looking for snacks and adventure.

'Duh DUH DUH duh DUH duh duh DUH DUH...'

'You can switch the music off now, guys,' I said.

But secretly I was kinda pleased. **99**

The End

'What a load of rubbish!' shouted the potato suddenly.

'Wuuaargh!' yelped Nancy. She jumped and the Talking Potato rolled out of her paw and onto the floor.

'Oh, how marvellous!' hooted Titus. 'You can actually talk!'

'They don't call me the Talking Potato for nothing,' said the potato.

'This is . . . weird,' said Willow.

'You think I'm weird? Well, little bunny, for what it's worth, I thought your story was completely ridiculous,' snapped the Talking Potato.

'Oh!' said Willow. Her ears drooped. 'That's a bit mean.'

'I just tell it how it is,' droned the Talking Potato.

'You liked my story, though, didn't you?' asked Titus, anxiously rubbing his hooves together.

'Utter codswallop,' sniffed the potato. 'Slow build-up, no action, boring lead character.'

'B-but I was the lead character!' said Titus, bursting into tears.

'Hey now, Spud,' said Frank, scowling at the Talking Potato. 'Titus here is very sensitive. You can't just dump a bad review on him like that, OK?'

'Fine,' the potato said, with a smirk. 'Why don't I tell you what I thought of your story?'

'Nah, you're all right,' said Frank.

'I thought it was boring, just like you.'

There was an angry quack. Ingrid had woken up.

'Darlink, I've had so many reviews I can't even count them. The thoughts of a talking potato are not going to affect me in the least!' she squawked.

'I bet you only got bad reviews,' said the potato. 'Because your story was useless. I hated it.'

Ingrid's eyes narrowed.

Nancy growled. 'Anything you wanna say to me?' she said with a glint in her eye.

The potato sighed.

'Well, I've saved the worst until last,' it said.

Everyone gasped.

Nancy chuckled.

'You've got the story-telling skills of a flea,' said the Talking Potato. 'A dead flea. There weren't any jokes, I didn't care what happened. I'd rather watch telly.'

'Yeah?' said Nancy. 'Well I'd rather eat some chips.'

The Talking Potato looked confused.

'Lovely, lovely chips,' said Nancy, taking a

frying pan out of her pocket.
'I could really do with
some hot, tasty chips.
Anyone else?'

'Oooh yes!' said
everyone else.
'Chips! Chips!
Chips!'

'Now, how do you
make chips? grinned Nancy.

'Nooooooooo!' cried the
Talking Potato.

But it was too late.

(Ten minutes later)

'Well,' said Titus, dabbing his mouth with
a handkerchief. 'I vote we do the chips thing
every year.

Well done, Nancy!'

'A pleasure,' grinned Nancy.

Ted and Willow had snuggled up together under a blanket.

'Ooh, I feel so cosy,' grinned Ted. 'Sittin' by the fire listening to stories might be my favourite thing.'

'It's mine too, young Ted,' said Titus with a yawn. 'It brings us closer together. I never forget nights like this.'

'Oh, everyone's got a story,' said Frank, toasting a marshmallow. 'You've just got to be interested enough to listen to it.'

'That is well deep,' nodded Nancy, scratching her armpit. 'Sorry I cooked the Talking Potato, everyone.'

'Oh, pshaw,' said Titus. 'Don't worry. It was the rudest potato I've ever met. And we don't need to hold a silly vegetable to tell each other stories, do we?'

'I hope not,' said a worried parsnip who happened to be passing. And so the friends sat around the warm glow of the fire and carried on sharing stories, hot chocolate and chips all night long. Until eventually, the sun rose up and bathed Grimwood in bright spring sunshine.

Oh, that was marvellous! If extremely silly. Honestly, who writes this stuff? Well, I'm off for a tour of a whelk museum. Byeeeeeee!

Happy
World Book Day!

As a charity, our mission is to encourage every child and young person to enjoy reading, and to have a book of their own.

Everyone is a reader — that includes you!

Whether you enjoy **comics**, **fact books**, **adventure stories**, **recipes** – books are for everyone and every book counts.

On **World Book Day**, everyone comes together to have **FUN** reading. Talking about and sharing books with your friends and family makes reading even more memorable and magic.

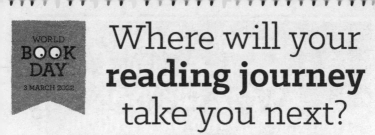

Where will your **reading journey** take you next?

1 Take a trip to your local bookshop

Brimming with brilliant books and helpful booksellers to share awesome reading recommendations, bookshops are magical places. You can even enjoy booky events and meet your favourite authors and illustrators!

Find your nearest bookseller at booksaremybag.com/Home

2 Join your local library

A world awaits you in your local library – that place where all the books you could ever want to read await. Even better, you can borrow them for **FREE**! Libraries can offer expert advice on what to read next, as well as free family reading events.

Find your local library at gov.uk/local-library-services

Scan here to visit our website!

3 Check out the World Book Day website

Looking for reading tips, advice and inspiration? There is so much to discover at worldbookday.com/getreading, packed with book recommendations, fun activities, audiobooks, and videos to enjoy on your own or as a family, as well as competitions and all the latest book news galore.

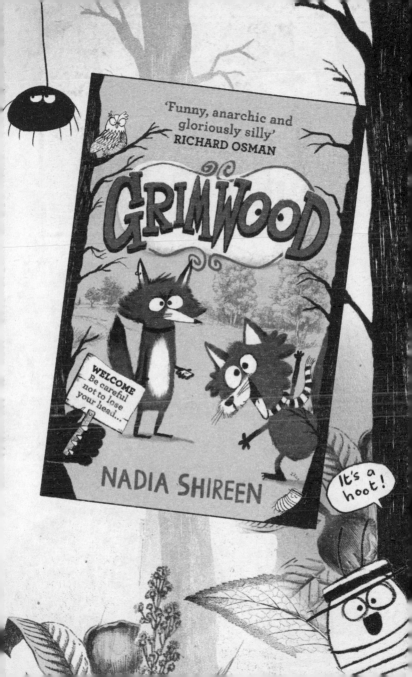

... AND THERE ARE EVEN MORE

GRIMWOOD

BOOKS COMING SOON!

This is the actual end of the book. No, really, this is it. There's nothing else. Seriously, go away. Love you, byeeeee!